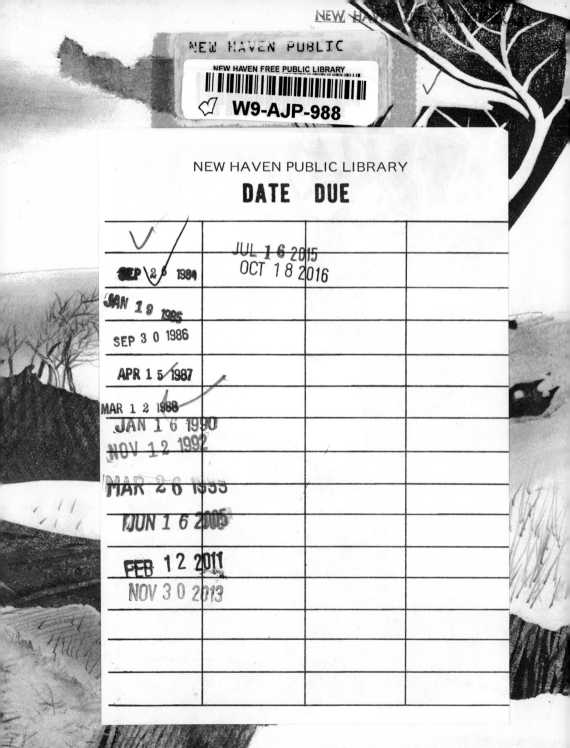

First Snow

by Helen Coutant
pictures by Vo-Dinh

FIRST SNOW

Alfred A. Knopf 🐎 New York

THIS IS A BORZOI BOOK PUBLISHED BY ALFRED A. KNOPF, INC.

Text Copyright ©1974 by Helen Coutant
Illustrations Copyright ©1974 by Vo-Dinh
All rights reserved under International and Pan-American Copyright
Conventions. Published in the United States by Alfred A. Knopf, Inc.,
New York, and simultaneously in Canada by Random House of Canada
Limited, Toronto. Distributed by Random House, inc., New York.
Library of Congress Cataloging in Publication Data
Coutant, Helen. First snow.
    SUMMARY: With the help of her grandmother and the first snow
she has ever seen, a little Vietnamese girl begins to understand
how death can be accepted as a natural part of life.
    [1. Death—Fiction.   2. Family life—Fiction]   I. Vo-Dinh, illus.   II. Title.
PZ7.C8327Fi[E]74-1187
ISBN 0-394-82831-3
ISBN 0-394-92831-8 (lib. bdg.)
Manufactured in the United States of America 4 6 8 0 9 7 5

To the Grandparents of
Katherine Phương Nam and
Hannah Linh Giang

Thương Kính tặng Ông Bà Nội,
Ông Bà Ngoại của Phương Nam Linh Giang

Everyone was expecting the snow. It was the second week in December and the hills around the small New England town were such a faded brown that Liên ached for them to be covered over: a miracle only the first snow would bring.

It was not so long ago that Liên and her family had come from Vietnam. They arrived in summer so that at first the new climate seemed little different from that endless, comforting heat of the tropics they had always known.

But with the passing of summer into fall, the cold grew steadily stronger. As the days shortened, Liên's grandmother, already old and weak, fell sick. The doctor came often. Liên knew her parents were worried and wished for the warm days to return.

Yet though she loved her grandmother and

knew the cold weakened her, Liên could not help longing to see the snow. When she went shopping with her mother, she looked at the clean wooden sleds impatient children had already put out on their porches. Their gleaming runners made Liên shiver. It seemed to her that the sleds waited for the snow too.

Liên spent the dark, late afternoons
showing her grandmother pictures of snow
in a big book. Together they ran their
fingers over the photographs until Liên's
hands almost felt the cold and her ears
filled with the roar of an icy wind. The
thought that any day now the snow might
actually come made her heart beat faster.

6

Finally on a gray and heavy morning, the
doctor, who had come more often than usual
this week to see Liên's grandmother, said
that snow would surely fall before dark.

7

He liked Liên and before leaving would always stop to speak to her. But today, as he turned up his collar against the bitter cold and pressed her father's arm, his face was less cheerful than usual. Her father and mother had followed him to the front door and now they stood silently. Liên watched through the curtains as he hurried away. Then she heard her father say to her mother, "Grandmother is dying."

Dying? wondered Liên. It was a word she had not paid much attention to before. Looking out the window at the frozen ground and the gray clouds, she asked herself if Grandmother's dying had something to do with the coming snow.

She ran between her parents. "What does it mean that Grandmother is dying?" she cried. Hardly had she spoken than Liên felt

9

herself picked up and held by them both. But though they pressed her close, stroking her hair, Liên could see that their thoughts were far away. So she asked, "May I light incense for Grandmother?"

In front of the table, which they had made over into a kind of altar, much smaller than the one in Vietnam, Liên took the lighted incense stick from her mother, bowed three times and pushed it firmly down into the incense holder. "What does it mean that Grandmother is dying?" Her question, rising softly like one of the fragrant threads of smoke from the incense, seemed to have no answer. Already her mother had moved to the altar and begun to murmur a prayer. For awhile Liên watched the burning incense. Then she tip-toed away.

10

Outside the closed door of the room where
her father had gone she listened. In a soft
voice she tried calling. "Papa, what does
it mean that Grandmother is dying?" No
answer came. She could not turn the handle
and walk in without permission, so there
was nothing to do but tip-toe back to the
front window and wait.

The cold, thick glass of the window burned

12

her fingers like ice. By now the clouds
had fallen so low they hid the top of the
nearest hill. It was hard to imagine what
the garden would look like after the snow
came and made everything white. If she went
for a walk would her hair turn white too,
as though she had suddenly grown old? Only
her grandmother's hair would not be changed
by the snow, for it had been white as long

as Liên could remember. Yet today, something about her grandmother had changed, for she was dying.

"Grandmother will know what dying means," Liên decided. She ran softly from the hall to the small corner room off the kitchen, where her grandmother lived in order to be near the family all day long. The room was hardly big enough for more than a bed, yet Liên thought of it as large and sunny. White and yellow chrysanthemums bloomed in pots on the windowsill.

Grandmother was lying on a wooden bed. Her long white hair had been neatly fastened with dark pins. A heavy quilt was pulled up to her chin. Many nights Liên had slept under the same quilt with her grandmother. Now she sat down on the bed, dropped her shoes to the floor and pulled some of the warm quilt over herself. Then she looked her grandmother in the eyes.

"What does it mean that you are dying, Grandmother?" asked Liên. Her grandmother

16

remained silent but she reached out from under the quilt and took Liên's hand in hers. "The doctor said the snow will come today," Liên said.

"So . . ." her grandmother whispered, "I think it has come just for us, Liên." Gently she turned Liên's head toward the window. Together they looked past the chrysanthemums into the winter sky. "This morning it is cold, my child, is it not? Heavy clouds are hanging over the pine trees. It seems that the whole sky is ready to fall and cover us with snow." She stopped abruptly. For a long time, Liên waited, wondering if the peaceful breathing of her grandmother meant she was falling asleep. Then in a clear voice, her grandmother continued. "Now listen carefully. If you

17

go out into the garden and hold your hand
up to heaven and are patient, you will have
an answer to your question. You will
discover for yourself what dying means."

"Then I am right!" Liên exclaimed,
sitting up, sure now that her grandmother's
dying had something to do with the first
snowfall. She pulled her legs out from
under the quilt, slipped into her shoes
and kissed her grandmother.

"Dress warmly, my child," her grandmother said. "And go right away. It would
be a pity to be late."

The buttons on her jacket were hard
to fasten. But at last Liên had closed the
front door behind her and was running to
the middle of the garden.

It was a bitter day. All morning the sun had cut through the massed clouds only once or twice. Overnight the cold had cracked the bare earth and the little brook had frozen over. The air stung Liên's face and her breath went up in white puffs like smoke. She looked up at the dark clouds that filled the sky.

20

Far above the tops of the tallest pine trees tiny snowflakes had begun to fall. At first they circled lazily, but when the damp lower air ruffled their edges, the snowflakes began to grow and fall faster.

When she saw the snowflakes coming, Liên remembered what her grandmother had said and held her hand up to the sky. "The snow!" she cried. She stretched her arm as high as the thick jacket would allow. A gust of wind rushed through her hair. Then one snowflake landed on the tip of her longest finger. It balanced there and Liên stared at it, not daring to breathe. This was not the cold, hard snow of the photographs but a tiny, fleeting thing, beautiful and delicate.

Then the sun broke through the clouds
and shone for an instant on the snowflake,
causing its white edges to burst into a

24

thousand tiny rainbows. "Is this what dying means?" marveled Liên, remembering why she was standing there. But as if that thought had made a change, the snowflake shrank. "Come back, oh please come back!" Hardly had she said this than the snowflake was gone. A tiny drop of water rolled down into her hand.

Liên stared at her palm, at the drop that was just water. Then it, too, began to change. It seemed to expand in the sunlight; perhaps it enclosed another world, like the paperweight on her father's desk. "Look, Grandmother," Liên called, turning toward the house. But as she moved, her hand trembled and the drop of water, lighter than sunshine, rolled off. It fell to the ground and was gone.

"Oh," cried Liên, going down on her knees. Searching for the beautiful drop, she scraped away layers of dead and frozen leaves. Her fingertips stung from the cold. But she continued to look until something poked against her palm. Where the water had fallen, a tiny pine tree now stood up in the sudden light. No bigger than her thumb, this little tree already smelled of deep, rich forests.

At that moment Liên thought she understood what dying meant. The drop of water had not really gone; it had only changed, like the snowflake, into something else. "You will change, too," Liên spoke to the tiny tree, "but not yet." Carefully she covered the little tree with its blanket of leaves.

Now as she stood up, Liên's hands stung.
She plunged them deep into her pockets and
looked again at the sky. On her upturned
cheeks a new snowflake landed and melted,
then another. "I understand, Grandmother,"
Liên cried, running toward the house.

29

The window of her grandmother's room looked bleak and cold as Liên stared up, too small to see over the sill. But the chrysanthemums bloomed as always, so yellow and clear they seemed to be out in the snow with her.

A tap on the glass startled Liên. At first she could see only the darkness above the flowers. Then slowly, as if the face were being drawn on the glass, her grandmother's features appeared.

Now she put one hand gently against the pane and Liên's hand rose to meet it from the other side. A quiet smile trembled on her grandmother's face.

"I'm coming, Grandmother," Liên cried, raising her arms as if to fly inside.

30

"I'm coming!" she said. And suddenly
the whole sky was filled with falling snow.

Note

Liên's family is Buddhist, like most Vietnamese
families. And one belief of the Buddhists is
that life and death are but two parts of the
same thing. However, Liên does not realize
this until that cold winter day when she sees
snow for the first time.

This might be thought of as a story about death.
But it is also a story about life. We are
grateful to the editors of Knopf for having
seen this and for their decision to make this
a children's book. In particular, we deeply
appreciate the sympathy and help given us and
our book by Frances Foster and Janet Townsend.

Helen Coutant and Vo-Dinh

Stonevale, Maryland
Easter 1974

About the Author and Artist

Helen Coutant and her husband, Vo-Dinh, have
written a book which grew quite naturally
out of a shared belief that many of the
ancient ideas and traditions of the Buddhists
can have meaning for all people.
   Though this is Helen Coutant's first book
for children, it is not the first time she
and Vo-Dinh have combined their energies as
writer and artist. She, an American, and he,
Vietnamese—they have worked long and hard for
peace, producing a newsletter, pamphlets, and
a book, *Cry of Viet-Nam* (Unicorn Press).
   Besides writing and translating,
Helen Coutant also teaches English. Vo-Dinh is
a well-known painter and printmaker; a writer
and translator too. He has illustrated many
books, including *The Magic Drum*.
   They live in an old stone house in
Burkittsville, Maryland with their daughters,
Katherine Phuong-Nam and Hannah Linh-Giang.